The Land of Possibility

by Rhonda Magee

Illustrated by
Diamond Dixon

AuthorHouse™
1663 Liberty Drive
Bloomington, IN 47403
www.authorhouse.com
Phone: 833-262-8899

Because of the dynamic nature of the Internet, any web addresses or links contained in this book may have changed since publication and may no longer be valid. The views expressed in this work are solely those of the author and do not necessarily reflect the views of the publisher, and the publisher hereby disclaims any responsibility for them.

Any people depicted in stock imagery provided by Getty Images are models, and such images are being used for illustrative purposes only. Certain stock imagery © Getty Images.

Scripture quotations are taken from the Holy Bible, New International Version®, NIV®. Copyright © 1973, 1978, 1984 by Biblica, Inc.™ Used by permission of Zondervan. All rights reserved worldwide.

This book is printed on acid-free paper.

ISBN: 978-1-6655-6758-9 (sc)
ISBN: 978-1-6655-6757-2 (e)

Print information available on the last page.

Published by AuthorHouse 08/17/2022

authorHOUSE®

Contents

Chapter One...1

Chapter Two 2

Chapter Three...4

Chapter Four 6

Chapter Five 7

Chapter Six 8

Chapter Seven 10

Chapter Eight...11

Chapter Nine 12

Chapter Ten...13

Memo: the book is titled The Land of Possibility!

My idea for the book is for it to customized by dates and times, places of the passing of loved ones' it may be published as fiction or non-fiction both. I was inspired by my grandchildren (Diamond, Dazzlyn, Davin) they will never get the chance to share any memories with their great grandparents here on earth, at Christmas or any of the holidays or any extraordinary events in their lives. The book also may be a teaching tool for numbers, colors, and holidays. This book is a sentimental, dialog of my tears and imagination; it can be used as an heirloom for families across the world.

THE LAND OF POSSIBILITY

By

Rhonda Magee

The Land of Possibility…

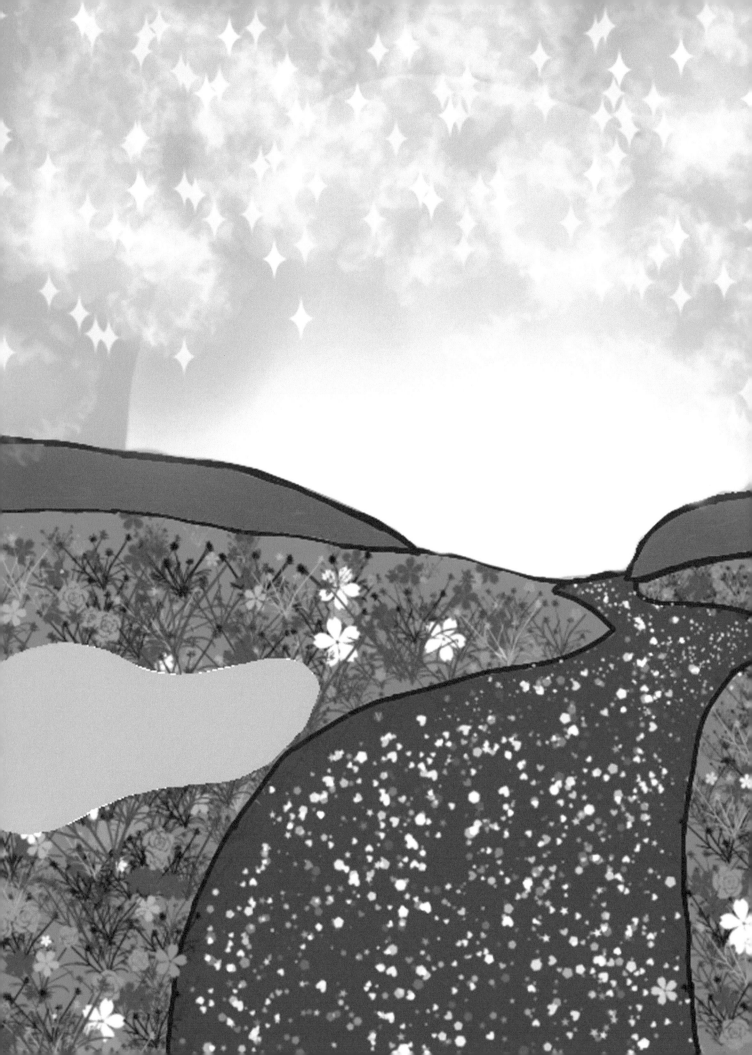

Dedications:

From the bottom of my, **heart** I dedicate the book to every little girl, boy, woman, man, who will never get the chance to feel the touch of their great-grandmothers etc. hands or hear the words I love you. To every dreamer, dreams do come true. To my grandchildren: Diamond, Dazzlyn, Davin, to my daughter Vanitee, you all are the reasons why I breathe.

In loving memory of my parents Perry and Johnnie Pearl Magee, my sister Ashley and my brother Perry Jr. Magee

And the God of all grace, who called you to his eternal glory in Christ, after you have suffered a little while, will himself restore you and make you strong, firm and steadfast. To him be the glory forever and ever. Amen.
1rst. Peter chpt. 5 v:10

Possibility - a chance that something might exist, happen, or be true

The Land of Possibility
Chapter

ONE

Once upon a time in the land of Possibility; there was a little girl by the name of Ashley Lashay. Ashley was born January 19, 1984, to, two loving parents named Perry and Johnnie Pearl Magee who loved her with all their hearts. The land they lived in was filled with beautiful flowers, magnolia trees, quite streams of the clearest blue water, and with the greenest grass; she had ever seen. There were sparkling brooks that trickled down a mountain, singing love birds, and beautiful butterflies flying all around her.

This little girl was made of sugar and spice and all things that are nice. Ashley loved seashells and puppy dog tails. She loved playing at her mother's flower garden with her puppy named Rainbow. Rainbow would give her a lot of kisses and sleep with her when she was feeling sad or lonely.

The Land of Possibility

Chapter

TWO

On October 28, 2007, an incredibly special Angel from heaven came to visit Ashley Lashay named Bertha. The Angel whispered in her Big Mama's ear and said, "come go home with me." Jesus sent me to get you because he need you to watch over special little girls here on earth who are filled with potential. The Angel also told her she needed her to help the Heavenly baker bake cookies at Christmas time, as well as to bake all the little girls and boys in the world birthday cakes.

So, Bertha said, "ok" she turned to her beautiful granddaughter and told her from the warmth of her soul; "I'll be watching over you everywhere you go, and I'll see you when you get to Big Mama's mansion in Heaven." I want you to be a sweet little girl, do well at school, love and obey your parents, as well as give your Gigi a lot of hugs and kisses, we will meet again one day. Ashley hugged and kissed her Big Mama and said goodbye; she also hugged her puppy Rainbow so tightly, dried her tears and she went off to play.

The Land of Possibility
Chapter

THREE

The sun was shining it was a beautiful brisk fall day. The leaves were turning orange and brown; they were falling ever so softly from the trees on to the ground. A few even fell on Ashley's head while her and Rainbow played. The squirrels were collecting nuts, the ants were securing food for the winter. The seasons were about to change. Although Ashley loved the spring, because everything would become alive and brand new. Such as the tress would begin to bud, the flowers, and the air smelled so refreshing. Ashley also loved watching the tiny little bunnies hop around while trying to keep up with their mothers.

One of her favorite holidays was Easter she and her Big Mama would dye eggs, cook up some delicious southern food. Summer is rather hot she thought; but the Fourth of July would be the next holiday favorite because of the fireworks but now summer have come and gone Fall is here. Ashley also noticed how the people she saw when she went into town were changing also. Most of them seemed so joyful and excited. The holidays were approaching now were Halloween, Thanksgiving, and Christmas.

"Wow", Ashley was so excited, family had begun to arrive from out of town such as Paris, Texas where her big momma grew up. Ashley would hear her Gigi say, "I sure hope we have a white Christmas this year, which mean she hope it snows. Ashley said to her Gigi at Halloween we had a hayride with dad, we camped out with family and friends, and we heard exciting, scary ghost stories. We roasted hotdogs, we roasted marshmallows so we could make smores in an opened fire.

Gigi, I was careful around the fire just like you told me to be. My dad Perry brought home this huge turkey, and mom told me the story about the Pilgrims and the Indians. Now, it is Christmas time Gigi, I am soooooo, excited. I love taking pictures, decorating the yard with dad. I hope Santa and his reindeers will bring me lots, and lots of presents; only if I have been a good girl of course.

The Land of Possibility
Chapter

FOUR

One day when Ashley was walking down the hallway at her Gigi's house; she saw a picture of this gentleman, she had never seen before. The man had salt and pepper hair, gorgeous gray eyes and he was hugging her Big Mama. She also saw this same gentleman pushing two little girls in a tire swing at this huge oak tree. She wandered where is he now? Well, her Gigi looked at her sister Tyla; and Tyla looked at her and they both said; "Shall I, or shall you?' Gigi said when the time is right, I will tell you all about your great-grand father Tom Magee.

Gigi said, we will have our conversations about your great-granddad Ashley; Ashley replied, "all right then, I'll be waiting," Ashley called Rainbow and asked if she could go outside to play? Ashley was sitting on the steps outside watching Rainbow run around in the front yard into the pile of leaves her dad had rack the day before. Then, all of a sudden Rainbow saw four squirrels playing at the yard. Rainbow began to chase after the squirrels. Ashley ran after him and said do not do that, "don't do that, it's just some cute little squirrels playing." But of course, Rainbow would not listen, and he kept right on chasing the squirrels until all four of them finally ran up a tree.

The Land of Possibility
Chapter

FIVE

Rainbow began to bark so loudly the neighbors came out to see what the noise is about. There stood this tall, dark haired, freckled face man with a short, skinny, red headed lady asking if everything was, ok? "Yes, ma'am its ok, it's just my silly puppy barking at a squirrel. The lady then asked, "where do you live young lady?" Oh, ma'am I live just five houses down, I am not far from home. Oh! "okay she said; may I help you with your puppy? But, before she could finish getting her question out, here comes this chubby, dark haired, rosy cheek little boy came running out of their house. He ran down the driveway and said, "What a cute little puppy!" "Hi" the little boy said to Ashley. Ashley said "hello", she picked up her puppy and started to walk home. She apologized to Mr. and Ms. Wigglesworth and said, "have a merry Christmas.

The Land of Possibility
Chapter

SIX

The little boy whose name was Max asked, "may I carry your puppy for you?" Ashley said, "no" I have him thank you. Rainbow did not like strangers he would snarl and snap at them when he thought strangers were trying to harm Ashley. Well, Max said then may I walk along with you? I was about to go play with my friend June Bug any way he lives about six houses down the street. Well, I guess so Ashley said. The two of them walked along in silence for a moment until Max asked, "What are you asking Santa Claus for Christmas Ashley?"

Ashley replied, "I really have not asked Santa for anything yet." I just want my GiGi as well as my mom and dad to be happy; the two of them will talk to Santa for me. My GiGi and I always at Thanksgiving go down to our church New Saint Paul Baptist to serve dinner to the homeless. I have a lot to do before Christmas comes Max. I am the one who gives the hot chocolate to them and my GiGi writes scripture on the cups to keep them encouraged. It seems to bring them joy. My family and I always do something meaningful during the holiday season, we give back to people because we thank God and love people.

The Land of Possibility
Chapter
SEVEN

My dad always told me how blessed we are. Mommy and Daddy sing to me at bedtime, we say our prayers together; and we ask Jesus to give seven presents each to other little boys and girls at Christmas. What are you going to ask Santa for June bug? I am going to ask him to allow my big brother Michael to come home from Iraq. My brother has been away for eight years now. I know my mom and dad would be so happy.

I have seen my mom's eyes sparkle like stars when he skypes on Saturday nights. My mother misses him terribly. I really do not know what I want for Christmas; a puppy would be nice. As they were approaching Ashley's house, she saw her dad Perry drive up with this huge green tree hanging from out of his truck. Ashley's dad honked his horn and called out for her; Ashley's dad yelled! Ashley walked faster and told Max and Junebug, "come on" my daddy's home.

The Land of Possibility Chapter

EIGHT

"Here I am daddy." I was just down the street; my silly puppy had chased this cute little squirrel, so I went to go get him. How was your day? Daddy you have been gone since eight o'clock this morning! "My day was great Ashley!" Daddy, while I was getting Rainbow; the neighbors came out from all the barking, and this is Max Wigglesworth. Max is almost nine years old, and he would like a puppy for Christmas. He plays with Dillion our neighbor; you have honked your horn at him several times for him to get out of the street.

The Land of Possibility
Chapter

NINE

Max walked up to her dad and shook his hand and introduced himself, "hello mister Magee," I am Maximillian Wigglesworth; I am almost nine years old, I'm very pleased to meet you. My mom and dad own Wigglesworth Jewelry. Have a happy holiday sir, "so long Ashley," Max said. So long Ashley replied. Daddy would you like for me to help you with this beautiful Christmas tree? Sure precious, just open the door for your dad. She rang the doorbell and called out for her Mother Johnnie Pearl. "Mom" Ashley yelled; dad is here! Everyone from the house came rushing out with such excitement from the family room to see this gorgeous tree. The freshly cut pine tree had already began to send a fragrance throughout the house.

The Land of Possibility
Chapter

TEN

The family was so excited Ashley's mom Johnnie Pearl asked if she would go up stairs to the attic; and bring down the rest of the decorations. Her mom had forgotten to bring the box down with the tinsels. As Ashley entered, she saw this beautiful glowing Angel, standing near the window. The Angel said, "do not ever be afraid to learn, from the least to the greatest." Anyone can teach you something no matter who they are. On your journey Ashley through out your life; you will encounter people from different walks of life; also from several countries. Believe in yourself, surround yourself with positive people. Never give up on your dreams. Be wise, LOVE NEVER FAILS! For God have a purpose for you. For all things are POSSIBLE, for those who believe. Merry Christmas sweetheart I love you!

THE END.

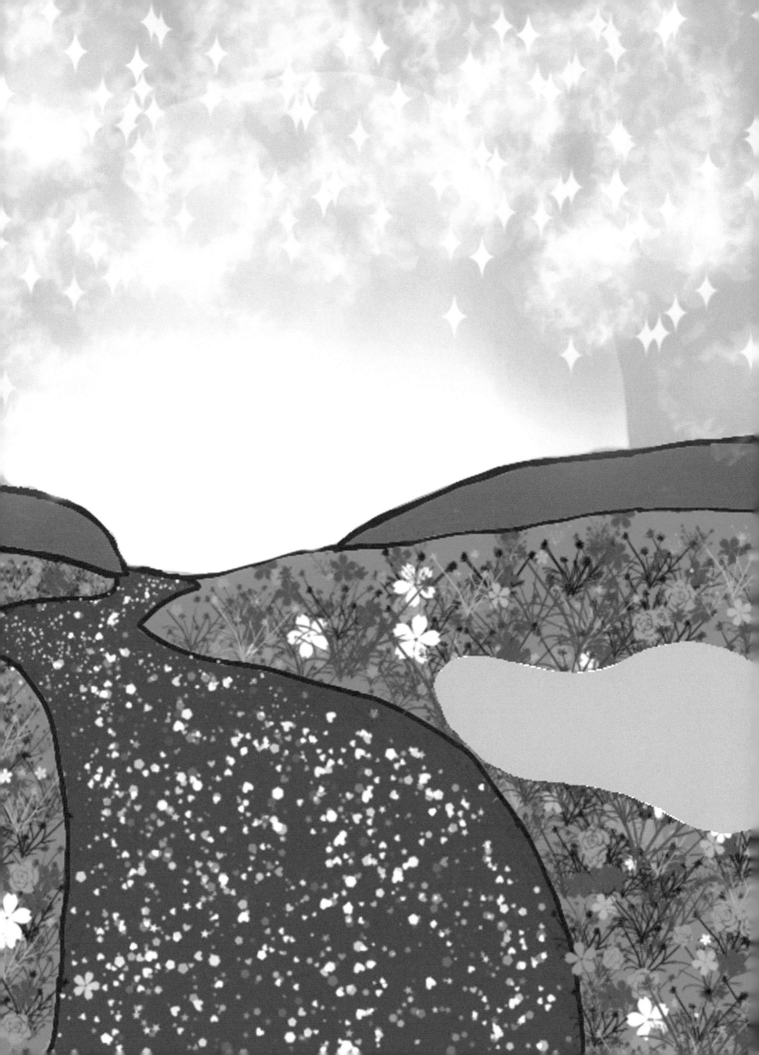

Printed in the United States
by Baker & Taylor Publisher Services